Maureen Bayless

Strike!

Illustrations by
Yvonne Cathcart

RAGWEED
THE ISLAND PUBLISHER

For Sue Ann Alderson, with thanks

Story Copyright © Maureen Bayless, 1994
Illustrations Copyright © Yvonne Cathcart, 1994

All rights reserved. No part of this book may be reproduced or transmitted in any form or by any means without permission of the publisher, except by a reviewer, who may quote brief passages in a review.

Ragweed Press acknowledges the generous support of the Canada Council.

Printed and bound in Hong Kong by:
Wing King Tong

Published by:
Ragweed Press
P.O. Box 2023
Charlottetown, P.E.I.
Canada C1A 7N7

Distributors:
Canada — General Distribution Services
United States — Inland Book Company
United Kingdom — Turnaround Distribution

Canadian Cataloguing in Publication Data
Bayless, Maureen, 1959-

   Strike!

   ISBN 0-921556-41-1

   1. Strikes and Lockouts — Juvenile fiction. I. Cathcart, Yvonne. II. Title.

PS8553.A745S77 1994   jC813'.54   C94-950062-3
PZ7.B38St 1994

Molly's mom was on strike.

All the workers in the union at the fish cannery were on strike.

This meant that Molly's mom wasn't getting paid much anymore, and she was worried and sad all the time. She'd even sold their television to buy groceries.

But the worst thing about the strike was that Molly missed her babysitter, Vi. Vi made the best hot chocolate with marshmallows in the world, and whenever Molly needed a band-aid, Vi gave her one with sailboats on it. Mom couldn't afford to take Molly to Vi's until the strike ended.

One day, Mom told Molly that they'd both have to walk the picket line.

"What's a picket line?" Molly asked, as she slipped Teddy into her backpack.

"It's a line of people on strike," said Mom. "We all carry signs called pickets that tell everybody why we aren't working."

"Why are you on strike?" asked Molly as they left the house. "I want you to go back to work so that things can be like before."

"I want to work, too," Mom said sadly. "I like my job and I need the pay. But our boss wants to cut back our pay, and we don't think we can afford to work for less. We decided to stop working so the boss will realize how much the cannery needs us and listen to what we have to say."

The fish cannery was at the edge of town, between the water and the forest. A few people walked back and forth in front of the cannery's three gates, holding pickets. They looked very tired.

"Hi, Kay," one of the picketers greeted Molly's mom. "My shift is heading home. There will only be two of you left because some people have the flu. But things are quiet."

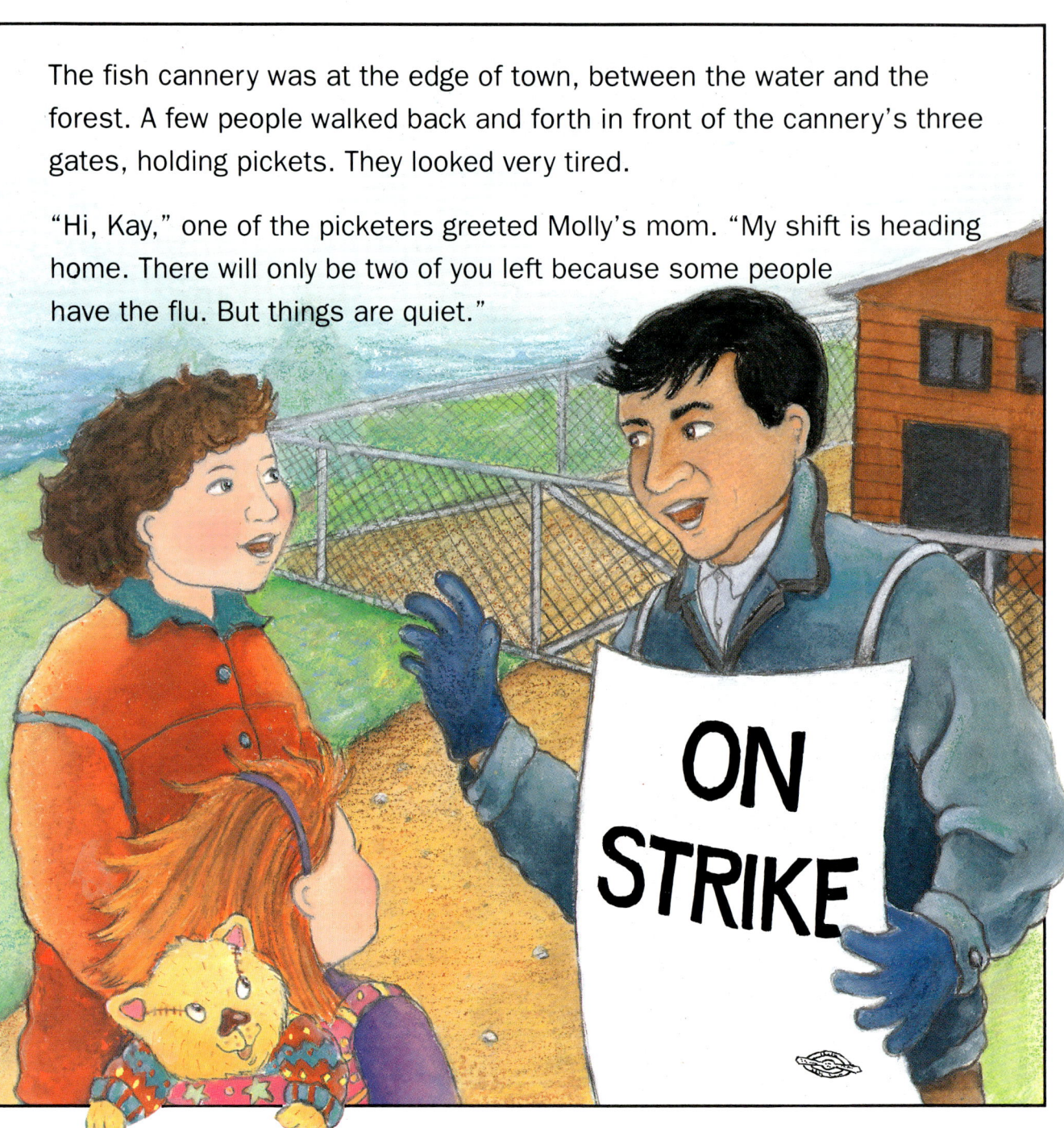

Molly picked up a picket. It was heavy, but she could lift it. "See Mom!" she said. "I can picket with you."

Mom smiled. "I wish you could," she said. "And I wish we had somebody to stay by that third gate. Truck drivers don't like to drive past picketers. If a driver sees that there is no one there, he might drive in and pick up a load of canned fish. If the fish is sold, the cannery will make money and the strike will last longer."

"Teddy and I'll go," offered Molly.

Mom gave her a hug. "Thanks," she said. "But we have to stick together. Besides, I'd be lonely."

Molly put Teddy in her backpack and dragged the picket down to Charlene's boat. "Charlene!" she called. "Can you help Teddy and me?"

"Maybe," answered Charlene. "But it's hard for me to leave the boat right now."

"That's okay," said Molly. "You won't have to."

Five minutes later, Molly thanked Charlene and carried the picket off the boat.

"Good luck!" Charlene waved.

Molly was secretly glad. She didn't really want to picket all by herself. She sipped the cocoa Mom had given her, and watched the boats rocking at their ties in the water. She could see Mom's friend, Charlene, painting her fishing boat. And way up high, an eagle was making a circle in the sky.

Molly had almost drifted off to sleep when she heard Charlene calling.

"I just had a call from Nelly's Café!" Charlene shouted. "A couple of trucks are headed this way to pick up a load of fish!"

A load of fish! Molly remembered what her mom had said. If the trucks took away the canned fish, the strike would last longer. Something had to be done about the gate that didn't have a picket.

Molly thought fast. "Can I have this?" she asked her mother, lifting one of the pickets.

"Sure," Mom shrugged. She went to warn the other picketer.

Molly dragged the picket to the unguarded gate. She leaned it against the gate, and put Teddy underneath, propping his arm up so that it looked like he was holding the sign. "You'll make a good picketer," she said.

Teddy looked so lonely that Molly almost changed her mind about leaving him. But she didn't. "Be brave," she called, and ran back to Mom.

On the way, Molly saw two trucks turn off the highway. They came down the hill, drove right up to Teddy's picket and stopped. The drivers got out.

"They're going to throw the picket aside and drive in," said Mom. "Maybe I should go over there. But I guess if I do that, they'll just come over here."

A car pulled up behind the trucks. "Hey! That car belongs to the *Bay Flyer* newspaper!" exclaimed Mom. "That's a reporter!"

The reporter hopped out of her car and took some pictures. After lots of talking, the truck drivers drove away. The reporter came over to Mom and Molly.

"That was a great idea," the reporter said to Molly. "Charlene phoned me about it. I was surprised, but it really worked."

"What worked?" asked Mom.

"Check it out," said the reporter.

Mom, Molly and the reporter walked to Teddy's gate.
They looked at the sign that Teddy was holding.

In Charlene's handwriting, in big, black letters, the sign said:

MY MOM HAS NO MONEY. MOLLY HAS NO BABYSITTER AND I HAVE TO PICKET INSTEAD OF PLAYING. PLEASE GO AWAY SO THAT THIS STRIKE WILL END SOON.
TEDDY

PLAY. FEW MORE DAYS. JOE AND FRANK

Underneath Molly's note, one of the drivers had written:

"Dear Teddy, Go home and play. We will stay away a few more days." It was signed, "Joe and Frank."

Mom swung Molly right off the ground. "I'm so proud of you!" she said. "You saved the strike!"

The next day, Molly, Teddy and the drivers were on the front page of the *Bay Flyer*. And not long after the paper was delivered, Mom got a phone call.

"My boss has called a meeting to talk about things," Mom told Molly happily.

"Does that mean the strike's over and Vi can come back?" asked Molly.

"Not today," said Mom. "Talking is just the beginning. But maybe soon."

Mom helped Molly into her raincoat. "Anyway," she said, "do you think I would leave you at home? I might need you. Just like yesterday."

"Teddy, too?" asked Molly.

"Teddy too."

Then Mom, Molly and Teddy set off to end the strike.